Yum Yum

You can read more stories about the gang from Buffin Street by collecting the rest of the series.

For complete list, look at the back of the book.

Yum Yum

Francesca Simon

Illustrated by Emily Bolam

Orion
Children's Books

Yum Yim first appeared in *Miaow Miaow Bow Wow*
first published in Great Britain in 2000
by Orion Children's Books
This edition first published in Great Britain in 2011
by Orion Children's Books
a division of the Orion Publishing Group Ltd
Orion House
5 Upper St Martin's Lane
London WC2H 9EA
An Hachette UK Company

1 3 5 7 9 10 8 6 4 2

A catalogue record for this book is available from the British Library.

ISBN 978 1 4440 0200 3

Printed in China

The Orion Publishing Group's policy is to use papers that are natural,
renewable and recyclable products made from wood grown in sustainable forests.
The logging and manufacturing processes are expected to conform
to the environmental regulations of the country of origin.

www.orionbooks.co.uk

For Martin

BUFFIN STREET

Hello from everyone

Lola

Millie

Miaow

Flick

Bow wow

Prince

Honey

Caw Caw

Do-Re-Mi

Snuffle
snuffle

Lily

Miaow

Joey

Rustle
rustle

Jogger

Miaow

Kit

Growl

Sour Puss

Dizzy

Bow wow

squeak squeak

Doris   Boris

Woof   Fang

Welcome to Buffin Street!

Come and join all the Buffin Street
dogs, cats, rabbits, puppies and parrots,
and find out what *really* goes on when
their people are out of sight...

"Lola!
Here kitty, kitty, kitty!
Yummy scrummy supper!
Come and get it!"

Lola yawned and stretched
on her red velvet cushion with
the gold tassels. She hadn't
moved from there all day.

Could she be bothered to slink over
to her bowl and see what boring old
food she was being offered?
She supposed she could.

Daintily, she sniffed at her
white china bowl with her name
painted in big beautiful letters.

Blecccch!

It was that revolting seafood platter in lobster jelly. No way was she eating that old slop again.

And yesterday had been
pheasant in gravy!
Phooey!

Lola was fed up with pheasant.
And tomorrow, I bet it will be
so-called succulent slices of salmon,
she thought, curling her lip.

I am sick and I am tired of
this same old stuff, thought
Lola, stalking off angrily.

There has to be better food
out there somewhere
and I'm going to find it.

Lola climbed up the fire escape and burst through Millie's cat flap. There was Millie, eating her supper in the tiny kitchen.

"Hi," said Lola. "What are you eating?"

"Funky Chunky," said Millie, looking up from her chipped bowl while Doris and Boris the mice scampered about nearby. "Nothing very exciting."

"Funky Chunky?" said Lola.
"Sounds good.
Could I have a bite?"

"Sure!" said Millie.
She was a little puzzled.
Lola's extra special, delicious food
was the talk of Buffin Street.

Lola bent down
and took a tiny
mouthful.

"Blecccchh!"
she said.

"It's so dry and crackly!"

"I know," said Millie sadly.

"Listen, Millie, you have my dinner,"
said Lola. "I don't want it."

"What have you got?" asked Millie.

"Boring old seafood platter
in lobster jelly," sighed Lola.

"Seafood platter in lobster jelly!"
gasped Millie. "Oh my!"

Zip!

Millie sped off before Lola
could change her mind.

Lola looked for a moment at
Doris and Boris. They did look
awfully plump and juicy ...

But no.

Millie wouldn't like it.
Sighing, Lola padded downstairs.

Fang was snarling away as he
gnawed on a bone outside
his kennel on the patio.

"What are you eating?" said Lola.

"A yummy bone," snapped Fang, gripping it tightly in his paws. "And don't think I'm giving you a taste!"

Lola looked at the muddy, disgusting bone. "I wouldn't want one," she said, stalking off grandly up Dizzy's stairs, her head held high.

Dizzy was guzzling his dinner.

"What are you eating?" asked Lola,
peering in from the fire escape.

"Doggy Delights!" said Dizzy.
"My favourite!"

"Could I taste one?" asked Lola. They didn't look very tempting, but she was feeling hungry enough to try almost anything. Moby Dick, the goldfish, was nibbling away at some very odd-looking food, and no one had ever heard him complain.

"Go ahead," said Dizzy.

Lola delicately ate
one Delight.

"Blecccchhh!
That tastes horrible!"

"Not to me," said Dizzy.

"Yum Yum!"

Surely there was better food
out there somewhere, she
thought, jumping onto the fence
overlooking the alley.

Lola never set foot in
the filthy alleyway.
Nose in the air, she strutted along
the fence towards Bert's Beanery.
Her tummy started to rumble.
Where could she get something
good to eat?

Ah, there was Sour Puss
gobbling up her dinner
at Bert's back door.

"Oh, Sour Puss," said Lola,
slinking up. "Any chance
of a taste of your…"

"Eeeyooooowwwfa!"
spat Sour Puss.

Lola was so terrified she
slipped backwards off the fence
and landed right in the alley.

Eeeek, she thought, picking her
way through the plastic bags,
empty bottles, and greasy wrappers.
What a horrid, smelly place.

There was no hope.
I'll just have to starve,
she thought sadly, leaping
back onto the fence.

Suddenly Lola smelled
something **wonderful**.
The tempting scent
made her pause.

What could it be?
Lola sniffed.
And sniffed again.

It couldn't be — but it was.
The irresistible smell was
coming from Bert's bins.
Lola stiffened. She certainly
wasn't going back into the alley.

Then she heard Kit, Joey
and Flick squabbling inside
one of the Beanery bins.

Lola took one step closer.

"What are you eating?"
asked Lola, peering
down at them.

"Yo, Lola!"
shouted Joey.
"Great stuff in here!
Fish heads, tuna tins,
and cheese rinds!
Yabadabado!"

Lola wrinkled her nose.

"Stop it, Joey,
that's my tin!"
howled Flick.

"No, mine!" yowled Joey.

"Mine!" spat Kit.

"MINE!" miaowed Lola.

And she dived head first
into the bin.

"Wowee!"

said Lola, cramming her
face with food.

"This tastes brilliant!
I haven't eaten anything
this good in years."

"Lola!" said Kit.

"Yummy!" mumbled Lola,
her cheeks bulging.

"Um, Lola," hissed Joey.

Chomp chomp chomp.

"Lola!"

screeched Flick.

"What is it?" mumbled Lola,
her cheeks bulging.

"Get away
from
our food!"
yowled the
alley cats.

What an evening!
A bedraggled, muddy, stinky,
smelly Lola sauntered home.
So what if a bath awaited?

Miqow
follow me

Did you enjoy meeting Lola?
Can you remember all
the things that happened
in the story?

What does Lola find in her food bowl?

And what did she have to eat yesterday?

What does Lola decide to do?

Who does Lola visit first?

Why is Millie puzzled when Lola asks if she can try her food?

What is Fang eating when
Lola sees him?

What does Lola think of Dizzy's
Doggy Delights?

Whose food does Lola like best?

For more adventures with the
Buffin Street Gang, look out for
the other books in the series.

**Meet
the Gang**

**Rampage
in Prince's
Garden**

Jogger's Big Adventure

Miaow
Miaow
Bow Wow

The Haunted House of Buffin Street

Look at Me